I love my teacher _____ because:

HarperFestival is an imprint of HarperCollins Publishers.

A Teacher Is the Greatest Gift

Library of Congress Control Number: 2019953353
ISBN 978-0-06-302000-9

The artist used pencil, charcoal, and Adobe Photoshop to create the digital illustrations for this book.
Typography by Chelsea C. Donaldson
20 21 22 23 24 PC 10 9 8 7 6 5 4 3 2 1

First Edition

A Teacher Is the Greatest Gift

By E. B. Cobbler

Illustrated by **Sarah Jennings**

HARPER FESTIVAL

An Imprint of HarperCollinsPublishers

A teacher is the greatest gift,

A flame to light my way,

An umbrella in a windy storm,

A big, bright sunny day.

A solid bridge that never sways,

A compass to help guide me,

An open book to magic lands

when the real one's far behind me.

A palette of colors to paint the world,

A language to help describe it,

Merci

Thank you

Grazie

Gracias

谢谢。

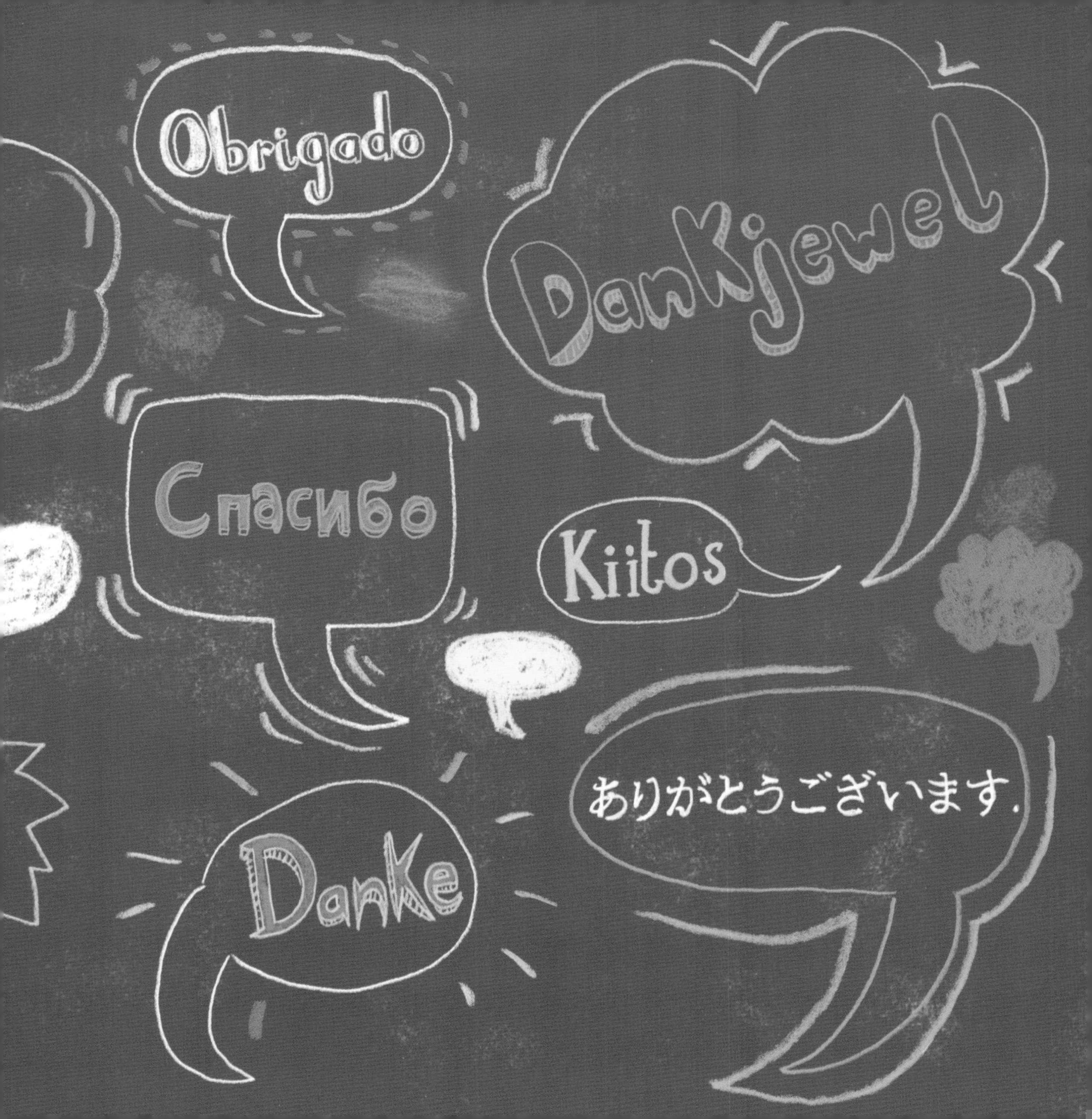
Obrigado
Dankjewel
Спасибо
Kiitos
ありがとうございます.
Danke

Numbers, shapes, and measuring tools

to help me build and size it.

Through all the ups and downs we share,

Through times of joy and tears,

A teacher's gifts stay with me . . .

long after my school years.